parents and caregivers,

Stone Arch Readers are designed to provide enjoyable reading experiences, as well as opportunities to develop vocabulary, literacy skills, and comprehension. Here are a few ways to support your beginning reader:

- Talk with your child about the ideas addressed in the story.

- Discuss each illustration, mentioning the characters, where they are, and what they are doing.

- Read with expression, pointing to each word. You may want to read the whole story through and then revisit parts of the story to ensure that the meanings of words or phrases are understood.

- Talk about why the character did what he or she did and what your child would do in that situation.

- Help your child connect with characters and events in the story.

Remember, reading with your child should be fun, not forced. Each moment spent reading with your child is a priceless investment in his or her literacy life.

GAIL SAUNDERS-SMITH, PH.D.

STONE ARCH **READERS**

are published by Stone Arch Books
A Capstone Imprint
151 Good Counsel Drive, P.O. Box 669
Mankato, Minnesota 56002
www.capstonepub.com

Printed in the United States of America in Stevens Point, Wisconsin.
042011   006170R

Library of Congress Cataloging-in-Publication Data is available on the
Library of Congress website.

Library Binding: 978-1-4342-2061-5
Paperback: 978-1-4342-2798-0

Summary: Buzz invents a special paint that
makes his skis go very fast.

Art Director: Bob Lentz
Graphic Designer: Hilary Wacholz
Production Specialist: Michelle Biedscheid

Reading Consultants:

Gail Saunders-Smith, Ph.D.
Melinda Melton Crow, M.Ed.
Laurie K. Holland, Media Specialist

BUZZ BEAKER AND THE SPEED SECRET

WRITTEN BY
CARI MEISTER

ILLUSTRATED BY
BILL McGUIRE

STONE ARCH BOOKS
a capstone imprint

Buzz Beaker loves to make cool new stuff. He keeps his ideas in a special notebook.

Larry is Buzz's best friend. He helps Buzz test inventions.

Vesa is a great skier. Nobody can beat her in a race!

Buzz Beaker is brilliant.

That means he is smart.
He is very, very smart.

Buzz invents things.

This is his super chopper.

This is his dog-washing machine.

Sometimes, Buzz's inventions work.

Sometimes, they don't.

Buzz doesn't mind.

"Good inventors never give up," he tells his friend Larry.

"Ouch!" says Larry. "I think my arm is broken."

Today, Buzz is making something really cool. He gets out the walrus oil. He gets out the butter.

He gets a secret ingredient from the garden.

He puts it in a machine.
The machine stirs it very fast.
Finally, it is ready. It is a secret
paint.

Buzz holds it up to the light.
"Perfect!" he says. "Let's go
try it!"

Buzz goes to the ski mountain to test his invention. Larry goes along.

Buzz pulls a paintbrush from his pocket. He takes out his paint.

"Oh, no!" he says. "The paint
is frozen."

Buzz thinks fast. Buzz thinks smart.

He warms the paint in no time.

Then Buzz paints the bottom of his skis. "This will make my skis go super fast!" he tells Larry.

Larry does not want his skis painted. "No way, Buzz," he says. "My arm still hurts."

The sky is blue. The snow
is deep. It is a perfect day for
skiing.

Larry and Buzz ride the
chairlift to the top of the
mountain.

Larry and Buzz race down the hill. Larry is slow.

Buzz is fast. Buzz is super fast!

He is passing everyone on the hill. Buzz is the fastest skier ever!

"My invention works!" he yells.

There is a ski race on the
mountain.

"You should enter the race,"
says Larry. "You will win for sure!"

A tall woman from Finland laughs when Buzz signs up. "No one ever beats Vesa!" she says.

"Who is Vesa?" asks Larry.

"Me!" says Vesa.

Buzz looks at Vesa. She is tall. She is fit. She is very used to winning. Good thing he has his secret paint.

The racers meet at the top of the mountain. They have fancy skis. They have fancy ski suits. They have fancy goggles.

No one can believe that Buzz is going to race.

The racers get ready. They get the signal. They go!

Vesa is in the lead.

But wait! Here comes Buzz!

Buzz jumps.

Buzz flies.

Buzz rockets down the hill.

Buzz wins!

"Hooray!" yells Larry.

Vesa falls on the snow. She sobs. Buzz helps her up.

"You are a good racer, Buzz Beaker," she cries. "I am no longer the fastest."

Buzz feels bad for Vesa.
She loves racing more than
anything.

Buzz loves inventing more
than anything.

Buzz gives Vesa his secret
paint.

"But be careful," he says.
"Don't let it get cold."

But Vesa did not hear him.

THE END

STORY WORDS

brilliant   mountain

inventions   frozen

inventors   signal

ingredient   Total Word Count: 459

LOOK WHAT BUZZ IS BUILDING!